KT-155-975

NOAH MAKES A BOAT
PIPPA GOODHART • BERNARD LODGE

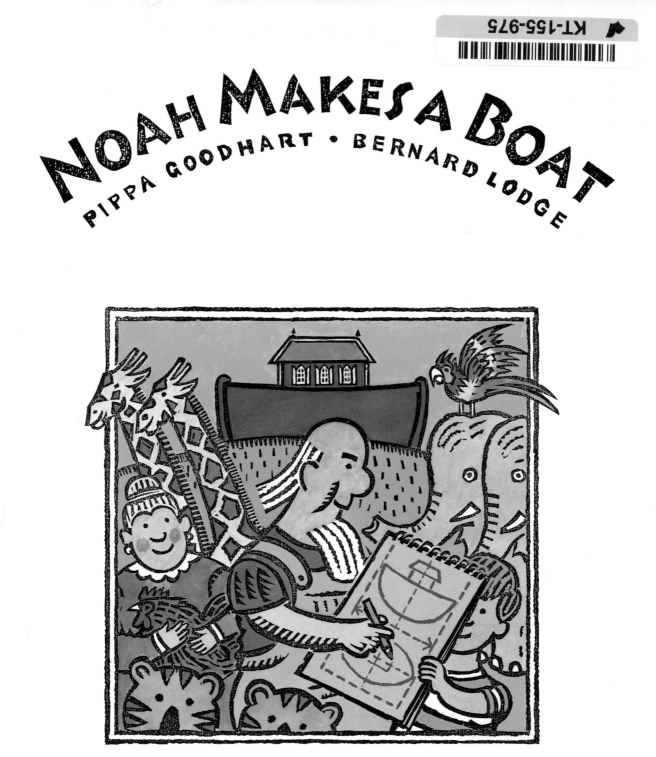

For William, the inventor
P.G.

For Benjamin
B.L.

SHETLAND LIBRARY

One night, God spoke to Noah.
'Noah,' he said, 'I'm going to send rain
and flood the land. I want you to make a boat.
Put two of every kind of animal into
the boat and keep them safe.'

'But I don't know how to
make a boat!' said Noah.

'Work it out,' said God.

Noah told Little Noah what God had said.
'Come on, then, Grandpa,' said Little Noah.
'Let's work it out. The birds floating on the
water must be the right shape for a boat!'
'They are all different shapes!' said Noah.

'But underneath they are all the same!'
said Little Noah.

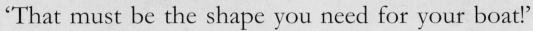

'That must be the shape you need for your boat!'

Noah drew his boat.

'What shall we make the boat out of?' he asked.

'Wood!' said Little Noah. 'Wood floats!

We could carve a boat out of a tree trunk!'

'But that wouldn't be big enough for all the animals,' said Noah.

Mrs Noah cooked fish for lunch.

Noah looked at the fish.

'That's it!' he said.

'My boat needs bones!'

'But how can a boat have bones?'
asked Little Noah.
'We'll make wooden ones, then nail on planks
of wood to keep the water out!'

Noah drew plans for the boat.
'What will we need to take with us?' he asked.
'There will be plenty of water to drink!'
said Little Noah.

'But what are we going to eat?' asked Mrs Noah.
'We can catch fish and the hens will lay eggs,'
said Noah. 'We'll have to take other food.
It needs to be a big boat!'
'We'd better do some measuring,
Grandpa,' said Little Noah.

Noah and his family built the boat.
They chopped and hammered
and sawed and nailed,
and the sun shone.

They collected and counted and stored
and sorted, and the sky got **dark**.

They led the animals up the ramp
into the boat, and it rained.
Splash! Splosh! Splat!
There were puddles, and it rained.
There were lakes, and it rained.

There was a sea of water that covered the land, and still it rained.

Noah's boat rose up on the water and floated.
'It works!' said Noah.

Then Noah yawned.
'There you are, God,' he said.
'I've made the boat and put the animals into it.
Now I could do with forty winks.'

God spoke.
'You've done a good job, Noah!' he said.
'You can have more than forty winks.
You can have forty days and
forty nights of rest!'

It rained and rained and Noah slept.
His family played 'I Spy.'

And then the sun came out.
The water went down and the boat rested on the
ground again. The animals and birds came out.

Mrs Noah hung out her washing and a rainbow
hung in an arc over the boat.
It was *beautiful*.

Noah drew his boat so that it would be remembered forever.

SHETLAND LIBRARY

And it was.

First published in Great Britain 1997
by Heinemann Young Books
Published 1998 by Mammoth
an imprint of Reed International Books Limited
Michelin House, 81 Fulham Road, London SW3 6RB

10 9 8 7 6 5 4 3 2 1

Text copyright © Pippa Goodhart 1997
Illustrations copyright © Bernard Lodge 1997
Pippa Goodhart and Bernard Lodge have asserted their moral rights

ISBN 0 7497 3422 1

A CIP catalogue record for this title
is available from the British Library

Printed in Hong Kong by Wing King Tong Co. Ltd.

This paperback is sold subject to the condition
that it shall not by way of trade or otherwise,
be lent, resold, hired out, or otherwise circulated
without the publisher's prior consent in any form
of binding or cover other than that in which
it is published and without a similar condition
including this condition being imposed
on the subsequent purchaser.